KELSEY the PURPLE BALLOONS

Candice L. Pyfrom

Copyright © 2017 Candice Pyfrom
Illustrations by Cameron Deangelo Johnson
All rights reserved. ISBN-13: 978-1502398192

For my Kelsey Bells

This is Kelsey.

She likes balloons.

Especially purple balloons.
Big, purple balloons
with sparkly ribbons
and green strings.

Kelsey likes to watch them dance against the bright blue sky.

She clasps the string, so long and green, while sparkly ribbons fly.

A playful breeze begins to blow, the balloons begin to sway. Suddenly she is rising — up, up, and away!

Up the long, green ribbon Kelsey climbs,
her magical balloon ride has just begun.

Sparkly ribbons glimmer and shimmer,
shining brightly in the sun.

The purple balloons begin to travel through the sky with ease. While birds in flight sing songs of delight, enjoying the sweet summer breeze.

The sun is shining brightly,
a cheerful shade of yellow.

The purple balloons jiggle and shake,
like heaping mounds of jello.

Kelsey soars high above the city, flying by the Nassau Straw Market and Linen Shop.

On Bay Street far below, policemen direct drivers to go, drive slow, and stop!

The Junkanoo festival is starting, Kelsey wants to join the fun! "Boom ka-lik, boom boom ka-lik."

What a grand sound goat skin drums can make! "Shook-a, shook-a, shook-a, shook-a," now the cowbells begin to shake.

Down Shirley Street the people gather, colorful costumes on display.

Kelsey watches from above, as the balloons continue on their way.

Perched high atop Fort Charlotte, old grey cannons make a handsome pair. Now on the lookout for pirates Kelsey shouts,

"ARGGHH mateys, beware!"

The balloons bob and weave towards the Ardastra Garden and Zoo. Kelsey marvels at all the animals below; there are iguanas, monkeys, parrots—and dancing flamingos, too!

The curious animals begin to jump and wave with such delight—
they whoop, stare, and point at the strange yet wondrous sight.

Kelsey spots a garden with tropical flowers on display.

Blossoms of hibiscus gather together, creating a radiant, sun-kissed bouquet.

Shy, young lilies dressed in white
peek out from their comfy beds.
While roses begin to blossom,
revealing petals painted red.

**Kelsey watches as the sky becomes
a sleepy shade of pink.
The big, purple balloons drift through
the air softly, into the clouds they sink.**

The busy street below is now quiet,
all the shops have dimmed their lights.

The purple balloons complete their journey,
as day steadily becomes night.

On her doorstep Kelsey lands,
home just in time for bed.

Down the long, green ribbon she
glides, ready to rest her weary head.

Such an exciting day for Kelsey,
after her magical journey through the sky.
She is tired now, finally all tucked into bed,
Kelsey closes her sleepy eyes.

Good night Kelsey.
Good night big,
purple balloons.

Sweet dreams of adventures
way up high, floating and rising
in the peaceful night's sky.

About the Author
Candice Pyfrom is an entrepreneur and children's book author from Nassau, Bahamas. She draws her inspiration from everyday interactions with her children and the beauty and vibrancy of life in Nassau. Writing has always been a creative outlet for her, a way to explore her own feelings and observations about life. This is her second book.

About the Illustrator
Cameron Deangelo Johnson is an illustrator and animator born in Nassau, Bahamas. He has contributed works to comic books, as well as art galleries at The Central Bank of the Bahamas and at the University of the Bahamas. Having obtained his Associate of Arts degree at The University of the Bahamas, Cameron is currently pursuing a Bachelor of Animation at Sheridan College, Toronto, Canada.

Acknowledgments
I would like to express my gratitude to Stephaney Davis for introducing me to the very talented Cameron Johnson. Cameron, I would like to say that you make me proud to be a Bahamian. Your talent, work ethic, and willingness to learn and grow during this process have been remarkable. Thank you for bringing this story to life.

To Shannon Fanuko, once again your work on the layout and book design made every image pop and brought the story together seamlessly. Thank you for this tremendous gift.

Finally, I would like to say a huge thank you to my Aunt Bonnie for her constant support and guidance. I can't thank you enough for helping to edit and publish this book for my Kelsey Bells.